The RACCOON TWINS

Written and photographed by Janet Everest Konkle

 CHILDRENS PRESS, CHICAGO

Library of Congress Cataloging in Publication Data

Konkle, Janet Everest.
☐ The raccoon twins.

☐ SUMMARY: A pair of raccoons set out to find their
mother in the woods and nearly end up in the zoo.
☐ [1. Raccoons—Stories] I. Title.
PZ7.K8354Rac   [E]   72-1465
ISBN 0-516-03568-1

Library of Congress Catalog Card Number: 72–1465

2 3 4 5 6 7 8 9 10 11 12 13 14 15 16 17 18 19 20 21 22 23 24 25 R 75 74

R.B. and R.T. were twins.

They lived in a dark safe nest
with their mother. The nest was deep
inside an old oak tree.

Every night the twins' mother
left the nest to look for food.

Every morning she returned.

"Someday," she told the twins,
"you shall go with me. Until then you
must wait."

R.B. and R.T. looked down on
the strange new world below them
and waited.

One morning their mother did not return.

R.B. and R.T. waited and waited.

At last, very slowly, they backed down the old oak tree.

They went into that strange new world. . .

and they were afraid.

Buzzzzzzzzzzz! Buzzzzzzzzzzz!
A bee flew over their heads.
R.B. and R.T. ran and ran.

When they stopped, the old oak
tree was no longer in sight.

They saw a rock.

"If we climb it," said R.B., "we might see our mother."

The rock was slippery with morning dew.

R.B. fell onto the soft green grass.

R.T. could climb the rock.
But his mother was not there.
Instead a turtle was sunning
himself.

"Have you seen my mother?" R.T.
asked.

The turtle said nothing. He
disappeared into his shell.

R.B. climbed onto some logs.

He looked and looked. He sniffed and sniffed.

He found some bugs.

He didn't find his mother.

"See what I found!" R.T. cried.
He had crawled into a strange-looking
box.

14

"That is my house," said a Siamese cat.

"If you are lost, you may stay here with me."

"Thank you," said R.T., "but we do not need a house. We do need our mother. Have you seen her?"

"No," said the cat. "Perhaps she is at the big house over there. Raccoons sometimes go where people live."

R.B. and R.T. found the big house.
R.B. chattered loudly. R.T.
climbed up the door. He looked in.

Someone screamed.
Suddenly the door opened. R.T.
fell to the ground.
Something big and prickly pushed
the raccoon twins away.

Just then a little girl came running.
She picked up R.B. She put him in
a bed with some dolls.

Then she tried to feed R.T. some milk.

R.T. snatched the bottle and ran.

R.B. jumped from the bed. He ran, too.

Suddenly two strong hands picked
up R.B. and R.T.

"Can't I keep them?" the little
girl asked.

"No," her father said. "They are
wild animals. They should not become pets.
We will take them to the zoo. Until
then we will keep them here."

He dropped R.B. and R.T. into a
basket.

But the basket could not keep them.

Once again R.B. and R.T. were picked up by two strong hands.

This time they were put into a cage with WIRE BARS.

"You will stay there until we take you to the zoo," the man told them.

R.B. and R.T. were very unhappy

R.B. hung his head. He wouldn't eat or drink.

R.T. climbed all over the cage.
He was looking for a way out.
He pushed his nose against the bars.
He rattled the cage with his claws.
At last some of the bars came loose.
Quickly R.T. slid through.
"Come," he said to R.B.
R.B. slid through the loose wire
bars.

Just then two hands picked up R.B.

He shivered and shook. It was the little girl. She hugged him tightly.

"You don't like cages, do you?" she asked.

"You won't like the zoo, either," she told him. "They have cages there, too."

She thought for a moment.

"I want you to be happy," she said.

She put R.B. down on the ground.

Together R.B. and R.T. ran as
fast as they could—
      away from the cage,
         away from the house,
            and away from the people.
The Siamese cat was waiting nearby.
   "I saw a raccoon down by the river,"
he told the twins. "Perhaps it is
your mother."

R.B. and R.T. raced toward the river.

Their mother was there.

They told her what had happened.

She said, "You are no longer babies. You have seen the world and learned its ways. Tonight when the moon is bright and the world is asleep, you may come with me."

And they did.

ABOUT THE AUTHOR

1970 was the year that Janet Konkle was honored in *Foremost Women in Communication* and *Who's Who of American Women.* An author, photographer, kindergarten teacher, antique collector and cat enthusiast, Janet is constantly on the move. She takes and develops her own pictures, is president of the Michigan Association for Childhood Education and travels extensively.

"I like to photograph animals, especially cats," she comments. "I often will get an idea for a book while watching and photographing them."